Tinker·Bell

The Essential Guide

Written by Beth Landis Hester

Contents

Introduction

Have you ever wondered how nature gets its glow? Who gives it light and color as the seasons come and go? Well, it's me, Tinker Bell, and my friends from Pixie Hollow. Only fairies and sparrowmen are allowed to see the magic that happens on our little island. But like I always say, rules are made to be broken. So, have a little pixie dust and come on in—I'll show you how fairies are born, how we live and work, and how we bring flowers, fireflies, waterfalls, and wonderful things to the world you live in. Do you think you have the magic to see inside our world? If you believe in fairies, I bet you can!

Tinker Bell

Pixie Hollow

At the heart of Never Land is a secret place named Pixie Hollow. In Pixie Hollow each season has a realm, where fairies work their magic to prepare the chilly winds, glowing leaves, fresh green sprouts, and sun-kissed blooms that are nature's crowning glory.

Never Land is home to mountains, mermaids, and never-ending childhood.

Winter Woods

The fairies responsible for the winter are experts in snowflakes, icicles, and chilly winds. They help bring winter to the Mainland.

Autumn Forest

A park in fall can seem like a sea of blazing leaves aglow with light—but each small detail is the result of a nature fairy's careful artwork.

Spring Valley

Preparing for springtime is one of the fairies' biggest jobs. Every flower bud, warm breeze, and rainbow must be ready to bring a burst of life and color to the Mainland.

Summer Glade

Nature fairies train crickets to sing in the moonlight, give fruit its sweetest flavors, and make perfect sun-kissed ponds in Summer Glade.

Pixie Dust Tree

The Pixie Dust Tree spreads its roots from the realm of Pixie Hollow to every magical corner of the land. It is here that new fairies are welcomed to join in the magic.

"Born of laughter, clothed in cheer, happiness has brought you here!"

Queen Clarion is the most beautiful and graceful of all the fairies in Pixie Hollow.

The Queen's Council

Kind but firm, beautiful Queen Clarion rules over Pixie Hollow. Her gentle manners set a peaceful tone, but along with her ministers they have serious work to do: preparing for the changing of the seasons, leading fairies to the Mainland, and keeping mischief makers in order.

The Minister of Winter is in charge of snowflake and frost fairies.

The Minister of Autumn hosts the Autumn Revelry.

The Minister of Spring is always there to see the Everblossom open.

Bringing warmth and light to the Mainland is the Minister of Summer's job.

Taking Charge

Queen Clarion and her ministers work hard to keep peace and balance in Pixie Hollow. Each minister is in charge of a season, and oversees all the preparations for the trip to the Mainland. But everyone looks to Queen Clarion for the final decision.

Fairy Folk

Fairies love to help nature come alive.

Part of what makes Pixie Hollow so magical is the wonderful variety of fairies who live there. Each fairy has a special job to do, and together, they make sure that everything looks and sounds beautiful.

Music Fairies

Music talent fairies play spider-silk harps, gourd drums, and reed flutes—all made from nature's finest materials.

Lyria's elegant, flowing dress is perfect for performing

Lyria

As a premiere storyteller and the star of the Fairytale Theater, Lyria uses pixie dust and her way with words to keep Pixie Hollow's legends alive.

Frost Fairies

These fairies seem as delicate as snowflakes, but are tough enough to help bring winter to the Mainland!

Fairies can hear Viola's call wherever they are in Pixie Hollow

Viola

As Queen Clarion's herald, Viola lets other fairies know when the Queen is approaching and delivers royal messages throughout Pixie Hollow.

Coming Together

Fairies of every talent love to get together, especially if it's for an Arrival Day ceremony. Each fairy in Pixie Hollow has their own unique style and personality.

Scout fairies and sparrowmen use their pinecone perches to look for hawks and other threats to Pixie Hollow.

Fairy Tales

Lyria might be the star of the Fairytale Theatre, but many other fairies help out behind the scenes. Light fairies set the atmosphere and music fairies help bring Lyria's stories to life.

Arrival Day

The first time a baby laughs a fairy is born.

On the wings of the wind, is how a new fairy arrives in Pixie Hollow. When the beautiful and kind Queen Clarion welcomes a new addition to the talent ceremony, all the fairies and sparrowmen of Pixie Hollow gather round to see what talent they will have.

A baby's first laugh is wrapped in dandelion fluff and carried on the wind to Pixie Hollow.

Terence brings a new fairy to life, with a cup of pixie dust.

Happy Beginnings

Tink's life begins at the happy moment when a baby first laughs. On a fluff of dandelion she floats to Pixie Hollow, where Queen Clarion and her fairies welcome her with kindness and pixie dust.

"When a baby first laughs, a fairy's life takes flight."

Tinker Bell tries
each talent, but in
the end the tinker's
hammer glows
brightest for her.

Talent Ceremony

Symbols of every talent surround the new
fairy. By finding the talent that is right
for them, a fairy or sparrowman discovers
where they will live and the role they will
play in the changing of the seasons.

Tinker Bell

She's adventurous, optimistic, hardworking, and full of big ideas. Although Tinker Bell tends to bite off more than she can chew, and her feisty fairy ways can sometimes land her in hot water, she always tries hard to put things right and be a kind and loyal friend.

With a sprinkling of fairy dust, tiny Tink floats on air.

"I'm a tinker. It's who I am!"

Tinkering

Tinker Bell is great at getting things to work in unexpected ways. That's what tinkering is all about: using the tools at hand to try new things and see what happens.

Lost things are great for tinkering

Bold and Brave

Tinker Bell is one fearless fairy. When something goes wrong, Tinker Bell is never afraid to fix it. Even if it means traveling to faraway lands and confronting troublesome Trolls.

Tidy hair is true tinker style

Tink's Traits

Tinker Bell is a creative and curious fairy. When Tink's temper starts to rise you can usually hear her trying to count to ten!

Tink tailored her own leaf dress

Friends

Rosetta, Iridessa, Tink, Silvermist, and Fawn don't always agree, but they're always willing to share their talents and help each other out when something goes wrong!

Tink's stone hammer

Green shoes match Tink's green dress

DID YOU KNOW?
When Tinker Bell arrived at Pixie Hollow, every fairy hoped she would pick their talent.

15

Tinker's Nook

Deep within Autumn Forest is a shady spot where magic happens. In Tinker's Nook, Fairy Mary and her tinker friends have the important job of building, fixing, and making tools to help fairies of every talent. Tinkers go out to make deliveries to other fairies, but this cozy hideaway is their home sweet home.

"Being a Tinker is never a bore!"

Store room

Babbling brook

Fairy Mary
As head of the tinker-talent guild, Fairy Mary is organized, firm, but fair, and proud of her tinker talent. She can be strict, but always believes in Tinker Bell.

Clank and Bobble
Clank and Bobble try hard, but when they set out on deliveries, things don't always go to plan! One thing they do get right is friendship. They always look out for each other and for Tinker Bell.

All in a Day's Work

Fairy Mary keeps her tinkers busy with orders from all over Pixie Hollow. You never know what you'll find on a tinker's table: rainbow tubes, magical stones, acorn buckets, pots and pans—or a brand new creation, straight from a tinker's imagination.

The Workshop

Beneath the light of the flower lamps, each tinker has a toadstool table to spread out their tools and work on their latest inventions.

Wheelbarrow

Mouse carts are used for deliverys

Lost Things

Broken toys and tools washed up from the Mainland are "junk" to Fairy Mary. But to Tinker Bell, they are wonderful tools, which give her the inspiration to make new inventions.

Silvermist

As a water talent fairy, Silvermist always brings an open heart and an upbeat smile to her work. With a delicate touch, she can make ripples in a stream or cast a shimmering mist into the air. Sweet Sil is always willing to see the best in others.

Silvermist is a graceful flyer as she flits from pond to stream.

Sil's hair is long and flowing like a river

Spreading Dewdrops

Silvermist is happy to share the tricks of her talent. But not everyone can carry a dewdrop as gently as a water fairy!

One of the hardest jobs for a water talent fairy is putting dewdrops on spider's webs.

Sil's shoes skim over the water

Water droplets must be handled with care!

DID YOU KNOW?
Sil knows how to talk to babbling brooks!

Heart of Gold

Kind-hearted Sil never hesitates to lend a nurturing hand to a friend. She might not always say or do the right thing, but she always means well.

"Ride the breeze, follow the waves..."

Home Sweet Home

Near a waterfall, in Stillwater Springs, is Sil's home. With a pretty petal roof and dewdrop windows, it's signature Silvermist!

A long, blue dress is sweetly elegant

The Peacemaker

When her friends are upset, calm Silvermist always helps smooth things over. Whether she's giving advice or just offering an understanding ear, Sil helps her friends see that a little patience can be the best way out of trouble.

A Water Fairy's Work

In a dress the color of a summer stream, Silvermist floats over water and air bringing precious water droplets wherever they are needed.

Iridessa

As a light fairy, Iridessa can capture sunbeams and carry light in the palm of her hand. She helps bring spring to the Mainland by melting winter's frost. She takes her work seriously and doesn't like to break the rules, but Iridessa is always loyal to her friends.

Sensible Iridessa loves her job as a light fairy.

"The last light of day! It's the richest light of all."

Sunny Disposition

Iridessa's outfits are as bright as the light she works with. She wears pretty, belted dresses made of sunflowers and yellow slippers to match. Her long, dark hair is always pulled neatly back to let her focus on the work she loves— and show off her sunny smile!

Sunny, satin slippers

Sunflower petals

Light Work

As part of her preparations for spring, Iridessa creates rainbows in the mist, then stores them away in rainbow tubes to carry to the Mainland. It's just one of the ways tinker technology help light fairies make magic!

Hair is braided in a bun

DID YOU KNOW?
No matter what outfit she's in, Iridessa always wears her signature sunflower seed.

Sunflower seed

Friendly firefly

Iridessa shows Tink one of her favorite tasks: giving light to fireflies, but Tink doesn't find it quite so easy.

Wonderful light

Beneath her sensible streak, Iridessa is a romantic who loves her work. She's proud of her talent and the amazing things light can do, from creating beautiful rainbows to making fireflies glow.

Fawn

With a gentle touch, Fawn offers a helping hand to all the furry, fuzzy, and feathered creatures in nature. Her casual style fits her animal-loving nature: She's always ready to leap into action wherever she's needed—feeding, training, or just cuddling the animals she cares for.

Fawn is confident, practical, and mischievous.

Animal Magic

Cheese the mouse, like all the animals in Pixie Hollow, knows that Fawn is as soothing and sweet as can be. As an animal talent fairy, Fawn can talk to animals and has a special knack for gaining their trust and helping them do their best.

Learning to Fly

To Fawn, nothing could be simpler than teaching a baby bird to fly. Her calm confidence helps encourage little ones to leave their nest for the very first time.

Tinker Bell isn't quite as confident as Fawn, when she tries to teach birds to fly.

Sturdy boots for tough work

Fall Flight

In the fall, Fawn warms up in a long-sleeved version of her regular outfit. As the weather gets chilly, geese fly south for the winter—and Fawn makes sure she's there to welcome home the tired flyers.

Hair is tied back in a pretty braid

Fawn's belt is made of pine needles

"I'll have breakfast ready for all the little fuzzies coming out of hibernation!"

Pants made of dried leaves

Fuzzy Fashion

Caring for animals requires some pretty athletic moves. Fawn wears her hair pulled back and short, comfy pants so she's ready to run, roll, and take on any critter challenge. This fun-loving tomboy is a true friend to "fuzzies" and fairies alike.

DID YOU KNOW?

Fawn has a great sense of humor, and loves a good prank!

Rosetta

Rosetta sees the beauty in nature. In fact, she helps create it! But she also knows a crazy scheme when she hears one, and this sassy fairy isn't afraid to speak her mind. As a garden fairy, she makes sure every petal is picture-perfect—and that not a hair is out of place on her pretty head.

Rosetta uses her artistic talent to give flowers their most beautiful colors.

Garden Fairies

As part of the garden talent guild, Rosetta and her fellow fairies and sparrowmen care for the seeds, flower bulbs, and delicate blooms that give each season its color and variety.

A Rosy, Cozy Home

Like many fairies, Rosetta lives in a flower home, blending in easily with her surroundings. Her rosebud house is her signature color—pink.

Rosy red slippers finish off Ro's look

Sophisticated hair is Ro's garden style

"Git along, little sproutlings!"

A single rose petal makes this pretty top

Rosetta uses a powder puff and her portion of pixie dust to give her cheeks a sparkly, fairy glow.

A layered and lovely rosebud skirt

Garden Glamour

It's only natural that a flower fairy values good looks, and Ro is no exception! In a pink, rose-petal dress, Rosetta always looks stylish and unwilted. Her genteel manners and sweet sayings are just as delicate.

DID YOU KNOW?

Rosetta artistically paints flowers using paint made from berry juices and pixie dust!

Lost Things

Fairies usually bring wonderous things to the Mainland. But from time to time broken toys, watches, and other manmade trinkets make their way from the Mainland back to Pixie Hollow. To most fairies, "lost things" are useless—but to Tink, they are valuable treasures!

With a little work, Tink rebuilds broken pieces into a beautiful music box.

Fairy Mary calls lost things "junk" and wants them out of her tidy workspace. But even she tried repairing the music box once.

What Could it Be?

Tinker Bell has never seen a spring or a screw before but she doesn't let that stop her. Discovering how these unfamiliar things bend, bounce, or fit together just takes some imagination and Tink's got plenty of that!

26

When Tink has to make a scepter she asks Terence to find something pointy. Terence comes up with a round compass, which hides two pointers inside.

Sometimes the missing piece that makes all the difference is hidden where you'd least expect it. Tink found the ballerina from the top of the music box under some leaves on the beach.

"Stuff gets lost and washes up on Never Land from time to time."

The sound of a bell makes a pleasant surprise.

Screws can turn a handle or tighten a joint.

A spring gives bounce to almost anything.

Treasure or Not?

The lost things that are so amazing to Tink are everyday objects to people on the Mainland. It just goes to show that anything can seem wonderful with the right attitude!

A perfume bottle has a handy squeeze-bulb.

The stern face on this coin gives Tink a giggle.

Tink's Inventions

*I*t's clear where Tinker Bell's true talent lies— tinkering! She has got a knack for figuring out how things work, and an imagination that never runs out of new ideas. Tink dreams up all kinds of tricks and tools to help her friends, and when Pixie Hollow is in trouble, her clever ideas just might save the day.

Fairy Mary keeps track of the tinkers' work on her seed abacus.

A Plan

When Tink discovers that springtime is in danger, she tries to help the best way she can—with a list of wonderful inventions. It takes careful planning, but Tink knows she can do it with the right tools!

Amazing Ideas

Tinker Bell loves combining lost things with materials from nature. Thanks to her tinker talent, she thinks up lots of ways to make the nature fairies' work faster and easier. Her bright ideas aren't always a success, but that won't stop her from tinkering!

An old glove and a perfume pump make a great seed collector.

Tink turns a nutcracker into a berry-crusher to make paint.

This paint sprayer puts perfect spots on a ladybug.

Stone hammer

Thorn scissors

Tools Of The Trade

Tinkers adapt most of their workshop basics from nature. With a little tinkering, simple objects can become useful tools.

Pussy willow paintbrush

Mortar and pestle

Springtime

While frost fairies sprinkle the Mainland with snow, everyone in Pixie Hollow is hard at work preparing for spring! Springtime Square buzzes with energy as fairies of all talents make sure the season reaches the Mainland on time.

Everblossom

As spring approaches, the petals of the Everblossom unfold in Pixie Hollow. The blooming of this magical flower is more than just a beautiful sight—it signals the beginning of spring on the Mainland.

Perfect Painters

Animal fairies take great care to make sure each ladybug is painted to perfection. It takes a steady hand and a good eye to make sure each insect looks its best.

Time to Dig

Rosetta and her garden fairy friends teach bulbs and sproutlings to nestle in fertile soil. With a sprinking of sunshine and water, these baby bulbs will soon grow into some of nature's most beautiful creations.

Flower Power

Spring wouldn't be spring without the gorgeous colors that fill every garden. How do flowers get such vibrant hues? Fairies, of course!

"Spring won't spring itself!"

A New Season

At the Queen's Review, Queen Clarion inspects the springtime preparations. The Minister of Spring makes sure spring arrives to the Mainland, no matter what!

The Mainland

The glowing face of the clock shows the fairies where to go.

At the start of every season, nature fairies set off on the long journey to the Mainland. As one season draws to a close, fairies transform every tiny detail in nature to bring in a new season. It's a big job, but to a fairy, there is nothing better!

"To the air, fairies! To the air! The Mainland awaits!"

Fairies at Work

For most of the year, fairies spend their time in Pixie Hollow, preparing for the chance to bring the seasons to life. But on the Mainland, nature fairies put their skills to work: bringing new color to leaves and flowers, stirring new ripples into lakes and ponds, and helping hibernating creatures rise and shine.

Animal fairy Fawn awakens sleeping chipmunks for spring.

Tink is amazed by the beauty of spring on the Mainland.

Seasons Change

To a human eye, the change from winter to spring seems like a miraculous transformation. But fairies know it takes a million tiny details to change each season.

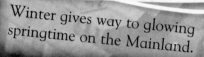

Winter gives way to glowing springtime on the Mainland.

Clank and Bobble help Tink make her delivery to Wendy.

A Springtime Surprise

A tinker's work usually keeps them in Pixie Hollow, but some seasons are full of surprises! Tinker Bell returns a lost thing to a grateful Wendy Darling—proving that nature fairies aren't the only ones who can bring spring to the Mainland.

Vidia

Fast-flying Vidia is one of the most gifted fairies in Pixie Hollow, and she wants everyone to know it! Hardworking and ambitious, Vidia takes every chance to show off her talent. But for the most part, she keeps to herself and steers clear of fairy friendships.

A high collar gives Vidia a stylish edge

Feathers keep Vidia flying smoothly at high speeds

Deep purple is Vidia's favorite color

Fast Flyer

Vain Vidia makes her talent look easy—but she's actually very proud of her ability to direct breezes, distribute pollen, and blow autumn leaves from trees. Vidia even uses her amazing speed to create whirlwinds.

One of a Kind

Vidia prefers to stand apart from other fairies, but in truth she has a lot in common with the other residents of Pixie Hollow: She is tiny, talented, and has lots of opportunities to learn from her mistakes!

Vidia's Schemes

Would an experienced nature fairy like Vidia let a little jealousy stand in the way of peace and friendship? Definitely! When Tinker Bell asks for help, Vidia finds a way to make her talented rival look silly instead!

When Vidia plays a practical joke on Tink, little does she know it might spell disaster for springtime.

"I am a fast-flying fairy. A true rare talent!"

DID YOU KNOW?

When Tinker Bell was a whisp of dandelion fluff, it was Vidia who guided her to Pixie Hollow.

Caught Out

Even fast-flying Vidia can't escape the watchful eye of Queen Clarion. When springtime is nearly canceled, the firm but fair Queen makes sure Vidia helps repair the damage.

Autumn

All of Pixie Hollow celebrates at harvest time, enjoying the seeds and fruits of nature before bringing autumn to the Mainland. The blue moon makes the fall festivities even more special than usual.

Fall's red and golden colors capture the light of nature.

Festival Lights

The light fairies raise glowing lanterns to set the stage for the Autumn Revelry, where all of Pixie Hollow gather to welcome in the beginning of the fall preparations.

Frog Song

Silvermist helps baby tadpoles practice their part in the celebration of fall, while Fairy Mary helps oversee the preparations.

The Moonstone

The moonstone is the key to Pixie Hollow's magic. Mounted in a scepter, it catches the light of the rare blue moon—and creates blue pixie dust, which restores power to the Pixie Dust Tree.

Tink's Scepter

Tinker Bell had a few problems making the autumn scepter, but when she puts her mind to it her scepter is the best yet.

"Nature's greatest changes come beneath the autumn sky."

Terence

Thanks to magical pixie dust, fairies can fly to faraway lands and lift heavy objects with ease. Every day, each fairy and sparrowman gets a fresh supply of pixie dust, to make the most of their talent—and pixie dust fairies are in charge of making sure there's enough to go around.

Wrist bands match Terence's outfit

Best Friends

Terence was one of the first to welcome Tinker Bell on her arrival day, and their friendship has grown ever since. Terence shares the secrets of Pixie Hollow, and helps show his friend how to be proud of her talent.

A satchel to carry spare pixie dust

Brown leaf leggings

Terence is never without his acorn cap

Fairy Gary

The leader of the pixie dust fairies has a big job to do—and Fairy Gary is just the sparrowman to do it! Fairy Gary's got his own style and he runs a tight ship at the Dust Distribution Depot, or "DDD" for short. But he's always glad for a chance to chuckle at closing time.

"Who's your best friend that always delivers?"

Flint, Bolt, and Fairy Gary work hard during their shift, but still find time to lighten the mood by teasing their friend, Terence, about Tink!

Pixie Dust, Anyone?

Handsome and hardworking, Terence is proud of his job as a dust keeper sparrowman. He gets to work with fairies of every talent, and he knows that his work helps bring magic to everyone in Pixie Hollow.

Boots made of cinnamon sticks

DID YOU KNOW?
The daily amount of pixie dust is one cup per fairy—no more, no less!

Cheese

Cheese the mouse is a faithful friend to the tinker fairies, and a big help around Tinker's Nook. He is always around to help carry a heavy load or to listen to Tink's problems. Nobody is sure how Cheese got his name, but he always comes when the word is mentioned!

When Tink and her friends have deliveries to make, Cheese pulls the heavy cart.

Loyal Cheese faces his fears to help Tink round up the sprinting thistles.

Faithful Friend

To a fairy, a mouse can seem like a giant! But bashful Cheese wouldn't hurt a firefly. In fact, he spends most of his time helping his fairy friends—from tossing lanterns to Iridessa to working the pedals of Tink's boat.

Blaze

*T*his little firefly has a big appetite! When he first meets Tink, he gobbles up her lunch, and she can't wait to be rid of him. But resourceful Blaze soon makes himself, and his light, indispensable.

Large wings help Blaze fly

Flashing tail

Tinker Bell meets Blaze on the way north of Neverland. Blaze doesn't make a good impression on Tink at first, but soon they are inseparable.

Fearless Firefly

Brave Blaze is just a baby, but he never shies away from an adventure or a chance to help his friend Tink.

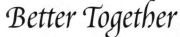

DID YOU KNOW?
Fireflies communicate with each other by flashing their lights.

Better Together

Even though Tink and Blaze haven't known each other long when they get into some sticky situations, the two friends realize how much they need each other.

41

Fairies' Friends

As caretakers of nature, it's no wonder that fairies have lots of animal friends. Creatures great and small depend on fairies and sparrowmen, and in return help bring cheer and comfort to Pixie Hollow.

Firefly

Fireflies are like eager pets to the light fairies, who give them their glow. They come when called and always have a friendly smile on their faces.

Ladybugs

Ladybugs trust nature fairies to give their wings a pretty red coat of paint and shiny black polka dots.

Butterflies

What would a fairy celebration be without a 21-butterfly salute? It takes a lot of practice, but these graceful flyers help see in every season with style.

Pillbugs

Pillbugs come to Tink's aid, when she ventures to the north of Never Land. They also play in the Fairytale Theater Orchestra.

Sproutling

Helpful sproutlings are good at following directions. When flower fairies ask them to, they wiggle into the soil and bury themselves ready to grow into pretty flowers.

Cricket

In Tink's house, a unique clock keeps fairy time—and a helpful cricket chirps when it's time to wake up.

Dove

When it is time to go to the Mainland, the Minister of spring rides ahead upon his graceful and fast flying dove.

Frog

Frogs take part in Pixie Hollow's animal orchestra, relax by Pixie Hollow's ponds, and try to stay out of the way when Tink gets into trouble!

Fairy Foes

Not everything in nature is a friend of the fairies—some of the most destructive and frightening creatures imaginable also lurk nearby.

Rat

Scary rats try and put an end to Tink's adventures north of Never Land. But with a little help from her friends, Tink manages to out smart these creepy creatures.

Trolls

As guardians of the secret bridge, it's the trolls' job to stop anyone from passing. But they're too busy arguing with each other to stop Tink and Blaze!

The Hawk

The hawk is one of the fairies' most frightening foes. Sparrowmen in special watchtowers sound the alarm whenever he comes near.

Sprinting Thistles

These destructive weeds are always trying to disturb the peace in Pixie Hollow. Nobody knows when they might come tearing out of the bushes!

Pack food
Pixie dust?
Warm clothes
Fly north
Find mirror

When Tink decides
to go to the north
of Never Land
she plans her
journey carefully.

Flying High

Tinker
Bell builds
a flying machine
out of vines,
and a cotton ball
sprinkled with pixie
dust. Terence's
compass will help her
find the way and her
new firefly friend, Blaze,
helps light the way.

North of Never Land

Due north of Never Land lies an island, which most fairies would not dare fly to. Unlike Pixie Hollow, which is a bright and happy place, the area north of Never Land is cold, dark, and mysterious. But for someone brave enough to find it, the island may hold wonderful treasures, too.

The journey to the north of Never Land is long and dangerous.

The Legend

Long ago perilous pirates found the mirror of Incanta, an ancient treasure able to grant three wishes. The pirates used two of them before their ship crashed—leaving one wish in the mirror's power.

Frightening trolls and other obstacles guard the shipwreck's location.

Whoever finds the mirror of Incanta can wish for their heart's desire.

Tink Forever

Tinker Bell's kind heart wins her lots of friends, but her quick temper sometimes puts those friendships at risk. A good friend has to be thoughtful, loyal, and willing to admit when she's wrong. It's a tall order, but tiny Tink can do it!

Loyal Clank and Bobble show Tink how to do a tinker's work—and to keep an eye out for each other.

"The treasure of true friendship will never lose its glow."

Tinkers Forever

Fairy Mary helps Tinker Bell realize what a talented tinker she is! Even when Tink ends up in a sticky situation, Fairy Mary never loses faith in her tiny tinker.

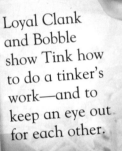

Working Together

Tinker Bell's friendship with Terence takes a bad turn when her temper gets the best of her. Luckily, Terence chooses to put his pride aside and help his friend Tink make the best scepter Pixie Hollow has ever seen.

The Best Tink

Outgoing Tinker Bell gets into some tight spots—especially when she lets her emotions run the show. When she learns to be honest with herself, and cool that hot temper, she is the best Tink she can be.

The Best of Friends

Iridessa, Rosetta, Fawn, and Silvermist are there for Tinker Bell when she needs them. Even if they don't always agree with her schemes, they're always available to give hugs, support, and to celebrate the good times together.

DK

LONDON, NEW YORK, MUNICH,
MELBOURNE and DELHI

Designer Thelma-Jane Robb
Editor Lucy Dowling
Managing Editor Catherine Saunders
Art Director Lisa Lanzarini
Publishing Manager Simon Beecroft
Category Publisher Alex Allan
Production Editor Clare McLean
Print Production Nick Seston

First published in the United States in 2009
by DK Publishing
375 Hudson Street
New York, New York 10014

09 10 11 12 13 10 9 8 7 6 5 4 3 2 1
175571—07/09

DK books are available at special discounts when purchased in bulk for
sales promotions, premiums, fundraising, or educational use. For details,
contact: DK Publishing Special Markets
375 Hudson Street
New York, New York 10014
SpecialSales@dk.com

A catalog record for this book is available from the Library of Congress.

ISBN: 978-0-7566-5512-9

Color reproduction by Alta Image, UK
Printed and bound in China by Toppan

Jacket design by Lisa Lanzarini.

Discover more at
www.dk.com